D0859614

To my son, Evan,
whose love for Kona inspires me.

    Karen

To my sweet dreams, Greg and Keli,
and my hanai sister Lauraine.

    Kimberly

In memory of Vonnie Lyons,
who left storyline notes for this book.

Also published by Mouse! Publishing:

Keikilani, The Kona Nightingale

From *Keikilani, The Kona Nightingale,*
the first in a series of books about Keikilani:

Most Kona's donkeys bray (hee-haw) at
night... which is a donkey's way of singing,
but it isn't very pretty. A few special donkeys
sing like birds. These donkeys are called Kona
nightingales. A nightingale is a bird that sings
beautiful songs at night. One of these special
donkeys was Keikilani (Kay-kee-law-nee),
which means child of heaven in Hawaiian.
She was called Lani for short.

    Vonnie Lyons

Published by Mouse! Publishing

P.O. Box 1674, Honolulu, Hawaii 96806

© 2009 Mouse! Publishing

ISBN: 978-0-9643512-1-9

Printed and bound in China

The Volcano Adventures of Keikilani
The Kona Nightingale

Written by Kimberly A. Jackson
Illustrated by Karen Dougherty Spachner

MOUSE! PUBLISHING
HONOLULU, HAWAII

Keikilani lives on a mountain
overlooking Kona, on the Big Island of Hawai'i.
Keikilani, or Lani for short, is an island donkey
and the people of Kona know and love her.

Life is peaceful for Keikilani,
a little too peaceful.
She is wishing for an adventure.

One day Lani saw a truck going to the town of Volcano, home of the only active volcano in the United States. The truck was going to pick up volcanic cinders for the gardens. Almost any plant will grow in cinders because of the rich minerals.

Keikilani thought,
"They're not going without me.
I've never seen the volcano
and I want to go!"
So she hopped into the truck
and off they went.

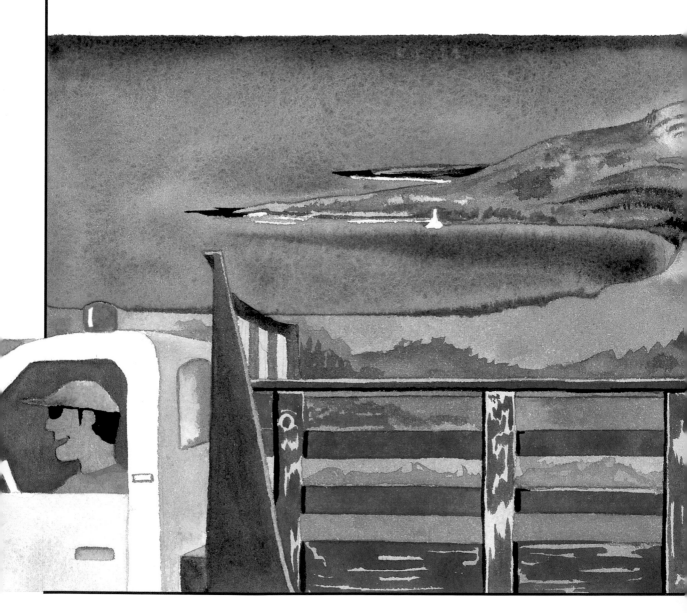

The driver wasn't concerned.
"Oh, look, there's our sweet Keikilani,"
he chuckled to himself.
"She won't cause any trouble."
Little did he know that Lani
was looking for an adventure.

When the truck parked at Volcano, Lani jumped off
and decided to explore. Kona has lots of lava fields,
but this lava seemed different. She poked her nose
in a pile of rocks and found a great big egg.
It wasn't like any egg she'd seen before.
She rolled the egg around and gave it
a little tap with her nose.

CRACK!

Out popped the most unusual creature Keikilani had ever seen!

"Thank you for rescuing me," the creature chirped.

"My name is Kana. I'm a dinosaur."

Could it be so?
The last remaining dinosaur on earth?
The egg must have been kept warm
in the volcano and finally worked its way
to the surface and hatched!

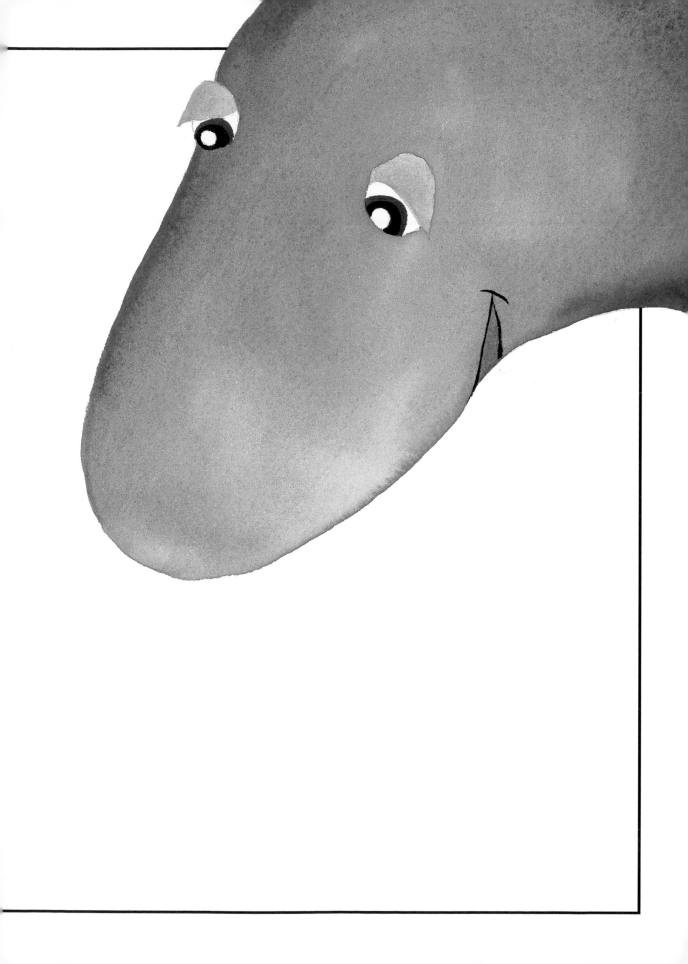

Keikilani stared at the creature.
For a baby, Kana surely was big.
Lani closed her eyes for a minute
in case she was dreaming.

She opened them and it seemed that Kana
had grown even bigger. And it was true.
Kana was growing bigger by the minute.

"What could Keikilani do
with a blossoming baby dinosaur?
"I have an idea," she said.
"We'd better look for Madame Pele,
the goddess of the volcano.
She'll know what to do."

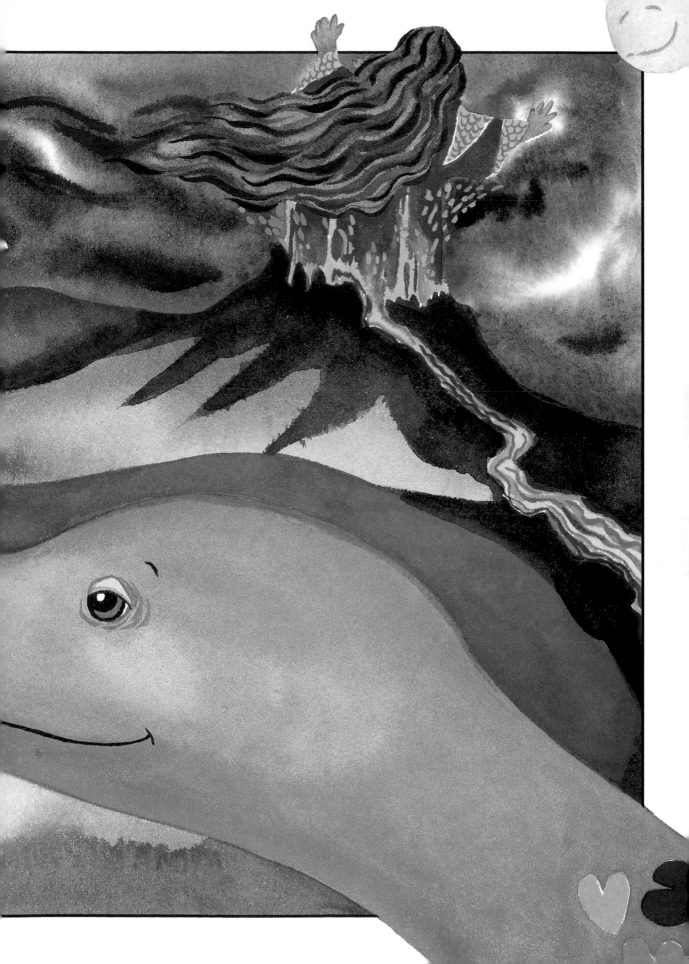

Madame Pele was easy to find,
for her home was the volcano.
Pele saw that Keikilani had a problem.
A dinosaur at Volcano would scare the people
and Kana was growing so big that he might
drag his tail across hot lava.

"Here's what we'll do," Pele said.
"I'll change Kana into a million geckos.
Geckos will be Hawaiian lizards, small versions
of their dinosaur relatives. Geckos will live
in every home in Hawai'i. They'll catch
mosquitoes and the people will love them!"

And with a wave of Pele's cloak,
Kana was gone and geckos were everywhere.

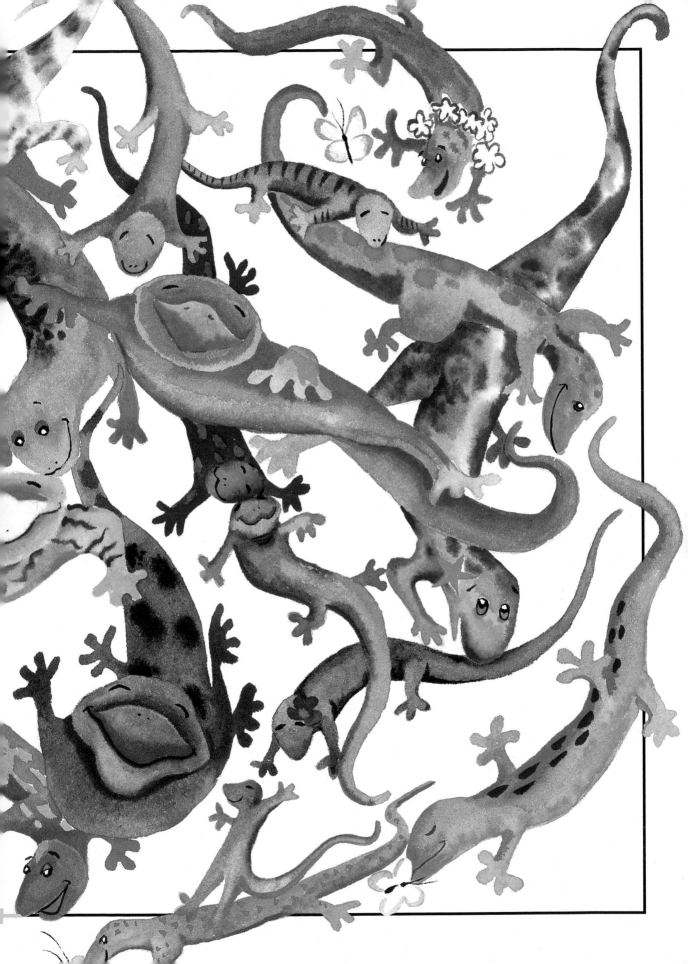

And off they all scampered,
except for one who nuzzled up to Keikilani.
"I'll call you Kana," Lani smiled.

So today there is no place in Hawai'i that doesn't have a gecko or two, squeaking a friendly cluck-cluck to let the people know they are there. And Kana traveled back to Kona with Keikilani and joins her in their nighttime lullaby. Sweet dreams, sweet dreams. Aloha and good night.